Ratatat   Hee Hee Hee

Text and illustrations copyright © 2017 Kate Alizadeh
Dual language and audio copyright © 2019 Mantra Lingua
The moral right of the author/illustrator has been asserted

First published in Great Britain in 2017 by Child's Play (International) Ltd
Ashworth Road, Bridgemead, Swindon SN5 7YD, UK

Dual language edition first published in 2020 by Mantra Lingua
Global House, 303 Ballards Lane, London N12 8NP
www.mantralingua.com

Printed in Paola, Malta MP101219PB01206661

A catalogue record of this book
is available from the British Library

MANTRA
LINGUA

Cicho, sza!
Quiet!

Kate Alizadeh

Polish translation by Jolanta Starek-Corile

SKRZYYYP

Creeeeaak

Ciii! Posłuchaj.
Co to za hałas?

Sssh! Listen,
what's that noise?

It's the bubbling of the pan
and the humming of the fridge.

W garnku
coś bulgocze,
a lodówka buczy.

HMMMMMM

Hummmmmm

and the clatter
from the sink.

BZYK

Whizzz

Stukam w stół,
a mój brat głośno beka.

It's me tapping on the table
and my brother burping loudly.

Tu kotek je swoje jedzenie,
a mój tata się śmieje.

It's the cat chewing her food
and my dad laughing away.

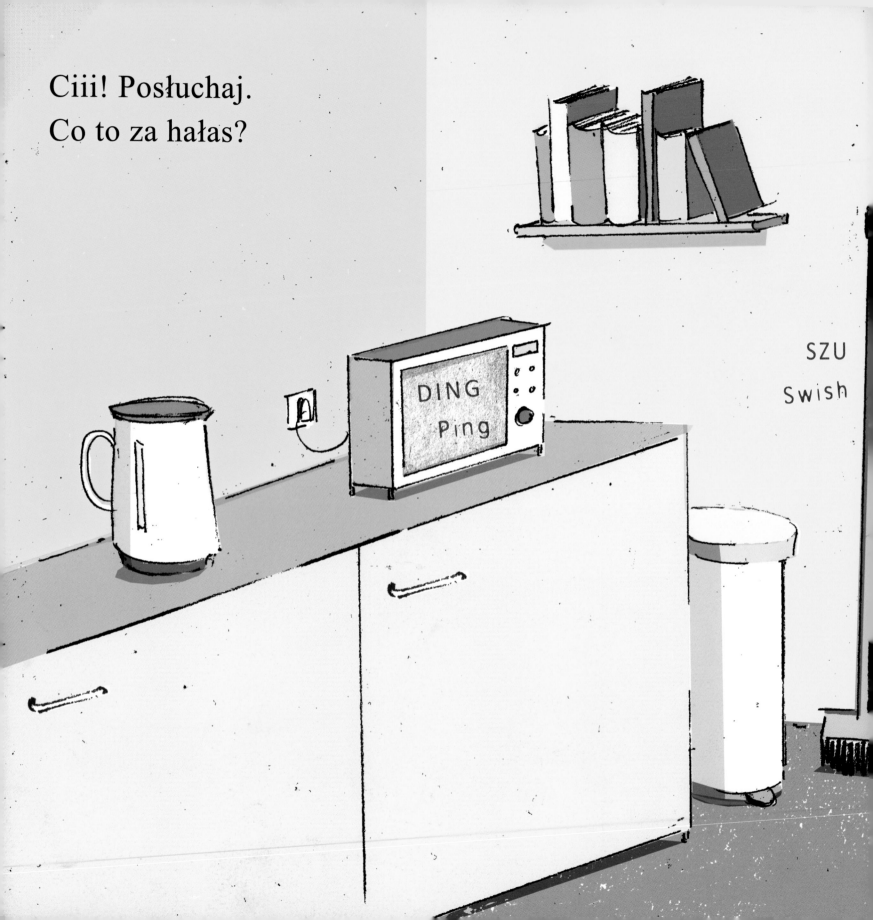

Sssh! Listen,
what's that noise?

W telewizji coś paplają,
kotek mruczy cicho, a ja śmigam
autkiem po całym dywaniku.

It's the TV babbling,
as I zoom zoom the car across
the rug and the cat purrs.

BLA BLA BLA
Blah Blah Blah

GADU GADU
Chatter

MRU MRU
Purrrr

BRUM
Brrmm

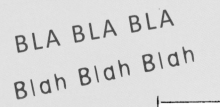

Piesek chrapie, laptop lekko furkocze,
a deszcz kropi za oknem.

And the dog snoring and the laptop whirring
and the pitter patter of the rain against the window.

Tu mój brat grzechocze zabawkami i chichocze,
jak gilgotam mu stopki łaskotkami.

It's my brother rattling his toys
and giggling when I tickle his feet.

Tak szeleszczą przewracane książki stronice.

And the swish and rustle as I turn the pages of my book.

Ciii! Posłuchaj.
Co to za hałas?

Sssh! Listen,
what's that noise?

It's the water dripping from the taps and the splish splash of my bath. And the squeak squeak of my rubber duck and the swoosh of the flush.

KAP KAP

Drip Drip

PIII Squeak

Woda z kranu kapie,
a ja chlapię się w wannie.
Tak zapiszczy kaczuszka gumowa,
a tu szumi spuszczana woda.

PLOP
Plop

SZYYY
Whooosh

Splish Splash
PLASK
PLUSK

Tak szumi suszarka do włosów.

It's the whirring of the hairdryer.

Szczoteczką ząbki szoruję,
a popłukaną wodę do zlewu wypluję.

And the scrubbing of my toothbrush
and the gurgle of the water down the sink.

Skrzypią deski od podłogi,
a łóżeczko trzeszczy.

It's the creak of the floorboards
and the bed squeaking.

To ściszony głos taty, kiedy do snu
czyta mi bajkę i niskim tonem cicho
nuci kołysankę.

It's the soft hushed voice of my dad
as he reads me a bedtime story.
And his deep quiet voice as he sings
a lullaby.

Idzie w klapkach klapiąc...

And the flip flop of his friendly feet...

a tak pstryczkiem robi klik
i na dobranoc całusa śle mi.

as he clicks off the switch.
And blows me a goodnight kiss.

Ciii! Posłuchaj, jaka cisza.

SSshh! Listen, it's so quiet.